Homework:

Write about a marine mammal that interests you.

For my mother and father,
who taught me love and curiosity

—CF

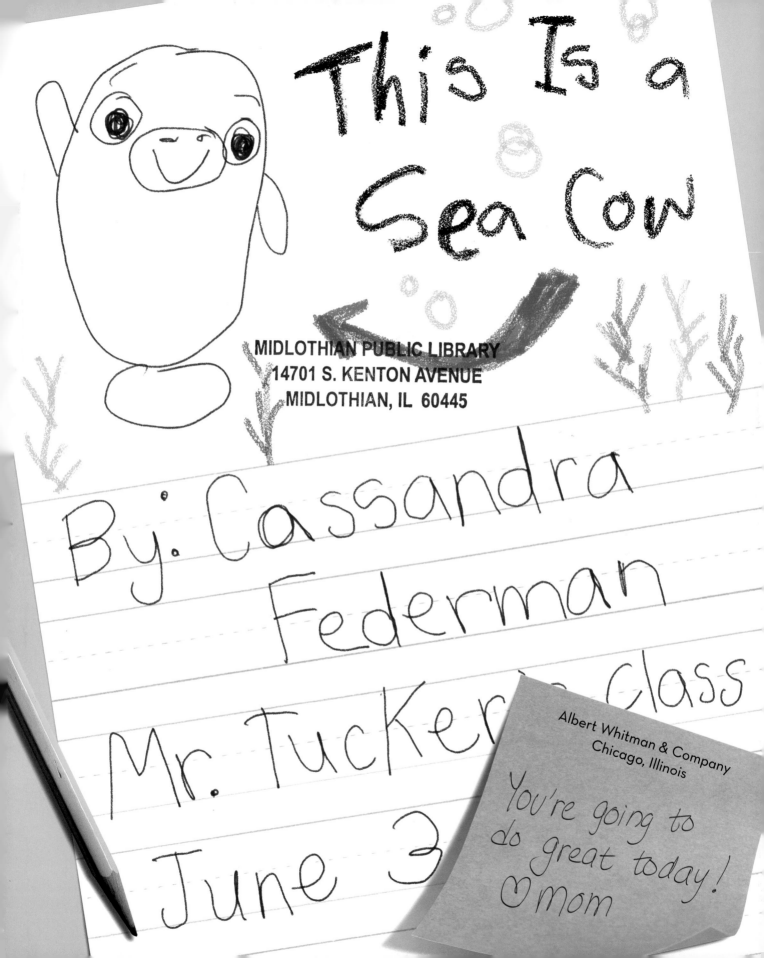

She eats grass like a cow.

She weighs over

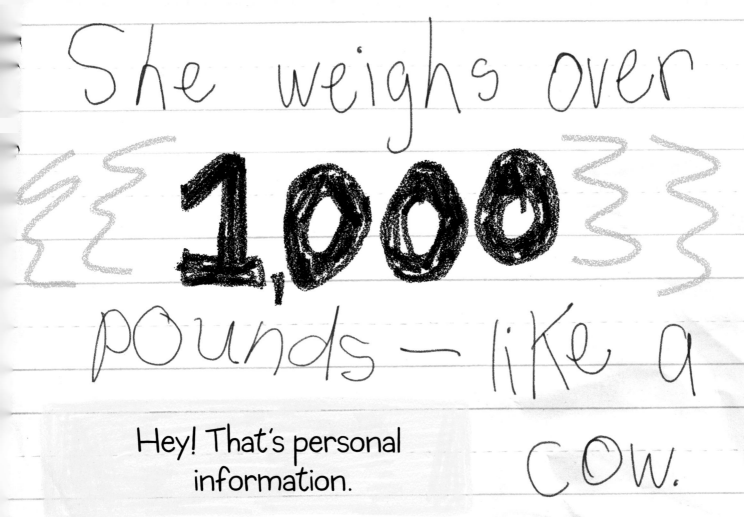

1,000 pounds — like a cow.

Hey! That's personal information.

And she gets gassy like a cow.

Underwater gas makes bubbles,

and everybody
loves bubbles!

the milk squirts
out of her
ARMPITS!

What's wrong
with armpit
milk? At least
armpits are
tucked away.
Cow udders
just hang
there—
GROSS!

Sea cows have little toenails on their flippers, but I guess that's not very cow-like.

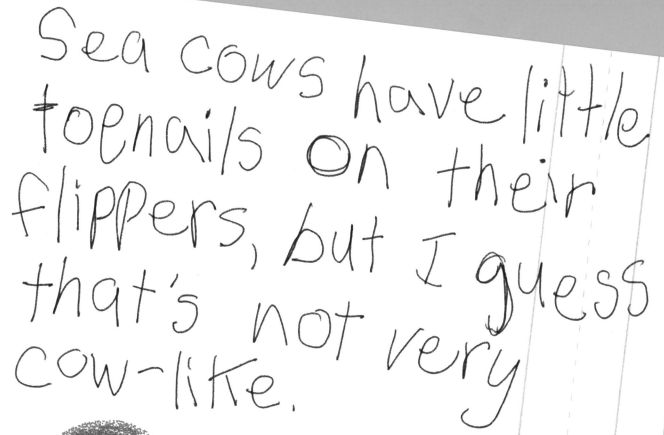

Maybe you should start comparing me to cooler animals. Like, did you know both manatees and SHARKS grow new teeth all our lives?

Wait— what are you writing there?

But an elephant's brain is so **BIG** that it never forgets. Sea cows have small brains.

X-RAY MACHINE

Hey! Who says I have a small— what were we talking about again?

Explorers probably had small brains too because they thought sea cows were mermaids.

A mermaid? Me?

are actually...

Please, pretty please,

...My new

FAVORITE ANIMAL!

CRAYON

Except for seahorses because they are a lot like land horses.

Ummm...
I don't think so.

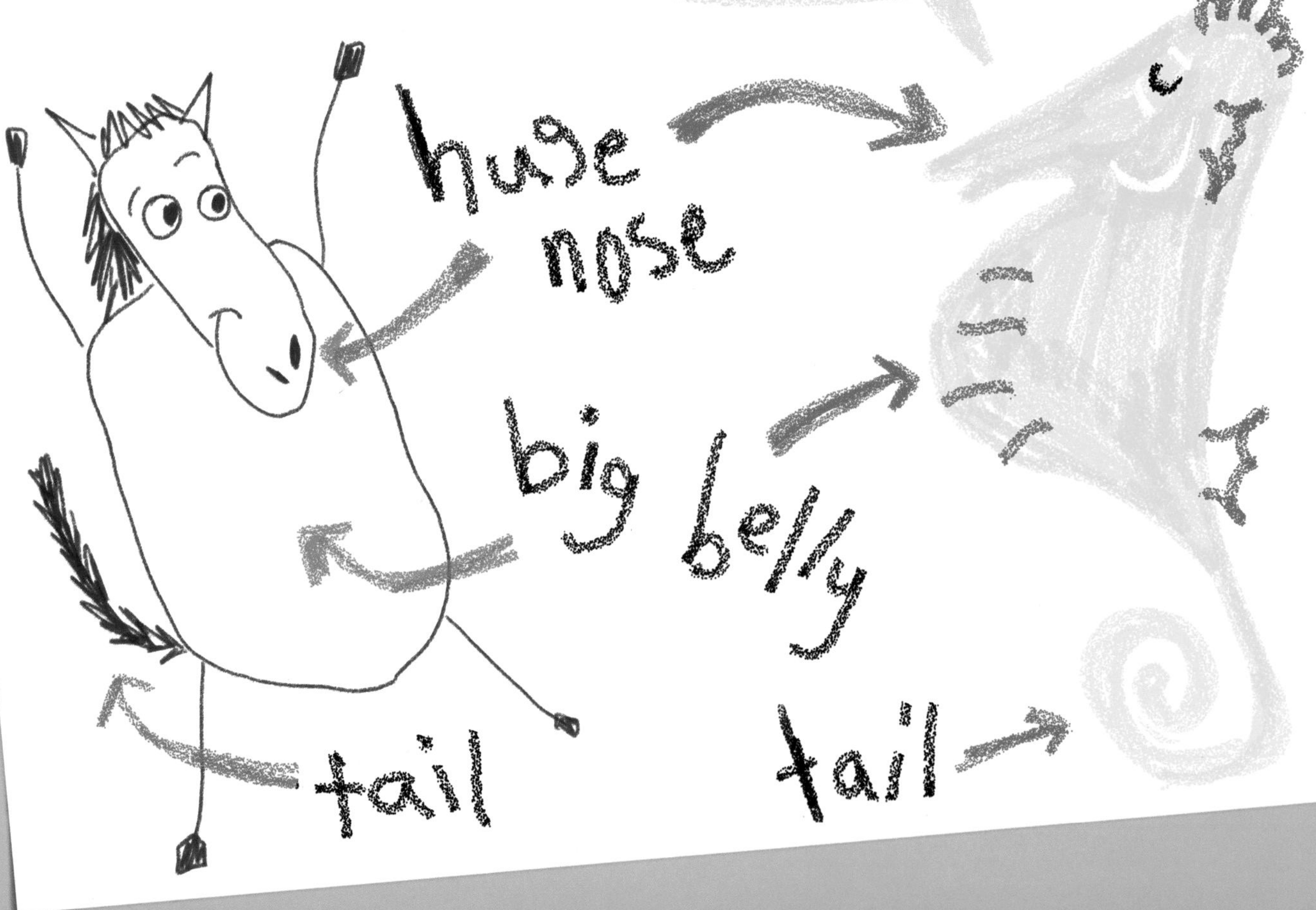

The

end.

Just for the record, land cows are *awesome*!

Hey, reader!
Here are some *cool* manatee facts that might interest you (NO cow stuff):

Even though we are heavy, manatees have very little blubber (fat), so we can't survive in water below 68 degrees Fahrenheit. That's why we live in warm vacation spots—like Florida!

Manatees can live for about sixty years! My *Nana*-tee is sixty-five. (She also lives in Florida.)

When I grow up, I'll be about 10 to 13 feet long. Standing on my tail, I'll be as tall as a basketball hoop. So I could totally dunk!

Manatees are herbivores, which means we only eat plants. I eat three bathtubs full of "Seagrass Salad" every day! Delish!

Manatees come up for air every three to five minutes, but we can hold our breath for twenty. How long can you hold yours?

Manatees can swim three to five miles per hour, which is the average speed that people walk. Manatees are a lot like people!

There are different types of manatees:

1. The West Indian manatees (that's me!) putter around the salty waters of Florida, the Caribbean, and the Gulf of Mexico.

2. The West African manatees are happy to hang in salty or fresh water. They go with the flow.

3. Then there are the Amazonian manatees. They only live in *fresh, non-salty,* water. So fancy!

Manatees don't have any natural predators.
(We even push alligators out of our way!)
But boats bump into us all the time, and their
propellers are sharp. Please look out for us!

In 2017, West Indian manatees
(like me!) were removed from the
endangered species list. Hooray!

YOU CAN ADOPT A MANATEE! (But we can't live in your
bathtub or anything, so we'll just send you pictures instead.)

Check out the adoption programs offered by Save the Manatee
Club and World Wildlife Fund by going to their websites.

You can also help injured manatees in Belize by donating
online to the Wildtracks Manatee Rehab program.

Library of Congress Cataloging-in-Publication data
is on file with the publisher.

Text and illustrations copyright © 2019 by Cassandra Federman
First published in the United States of America
in 2019 by Albert Whitman & Company
ISBN 978-0-8075-7874-2 (hardcover)
ISBN 978-0-8075-7866-7 (ebook)

Printed in China
10 9 8 7 6 5 4 3 2 1 WKT 24 23 22 21 20 19

Design by Cassandra Federman and Aphee Messer

For more information about Albert Whitman & Company,
visit our website at www.albertwhitman.com.

100 Years of Albert Whitman & Company
Celebrate with us in 2019!

Class Report Roundup:
What did we learn?

- Sea cows are different from land cows.

- Not all blue whales are sad whales.

- Walruses aren't just seals with big teeth.

by BERNARD WABER

Lyle, Lyle, Crocodile

Houghton Mifflin Company, Boston

for Mary K.

Printed in the United States of America

ISBN 0-395-16995-X Reinforced Edition
ISBN 0-395-13720-9 Sandpiper Paperbound Edition

HOR 30 29

NO
STANDING
8AM·6PM

This is the house.
The house on
East 88th Street.
Mr. and Mrs. Primm
and their son Joshua
live in the house
on East 88th Street.
So does Lyle.
Listen:
SWISH, SWASH,
SPLASH, SWOOSH!
That's Lyle . . .

Lyle the crocodile.

Lyle was very happy living with the Primm family.

He was especially happy when he was being useful . . .
like helping Joshua brush up on school work.

ut if Lyle was happy, he was making someone
se unhappy; perfectly miserable in fact.
hat someone else was Loretta, Mr. Grumps' cat.
r. Grumps lived just two houses away from the Primms.
henever his cat caught even the slightest glimpse
Lyle, she would fling herself into a nervous fit.

To take his mind off his troubles
with Loretta and Mr. Grumps, Lyle filled
his days playing with Joshua and his friends.
He loved being "it."

He could skip double-dutch
one hundred times without missing.

It came as no particular surprise
that Lyle could high-jump.
But Loretta, who was just let
out for an airing, was surprised.
She was terribly surprised.

Loretta was so surprised
and so shaken, she fled to
the nearest tree and
no amount of coaxing would
bring her down. Not until
Mr. Grumps arrived to
rescue and comfort her,
would she consider
coming down.

14

"Something will have to be done about
that crocodile," stormed Mr. Grumps.
Now Mr. Grumps was really furious.
Now he knew he would be snappy, irritable
and impossible to live with when he
returned to his job in a big department
store the following day.

For the next several days Mrs. Primm thought it best
to keep Lyle close at her side.
Together they fussed about the kitchen, preparing
good things for the family to eat.

When the weather permitted,
they took lunch to the park.

Lyle was always one for sharing.

They even took trips downtown.
There was much to see in the big city . . .
and much to do.

Mrs. Primm could spend hours
just browsing around antique shops.

Lyle could spend hours
watching building construction.

They both loved to ice-skate.

One day Mrs. Primm and Lyle went shopping
in a big department store. Unfortunately for
everyone, it turned out to be the very same store
in which Mr. Grumps held an important position.

And unfortunately, they were to hear from Mr.
Grumps all too soon. For it was his voice that
suddenly broke in over the loudspeaker to announce
a sale in the pajama department.

Immediately, it was as if everyone in the store
was in desperate need of pajamas.
Separated from Mrs. Primm, Lyle was
swept along with the crowd.

As they neared the pajama department,
Lyle thought he heard a familiar voice.
"Lyle, Lyle," the voice called out.
Lyle recognized the voice all right . . .

. . . and the face as well.
The voice and the face belonged to
Hector P. Valenti, star of stage and screen.
But what was Signor Valenti up to now?
Well, for the moment it seemed,
he was very busy selling pajamas.

Lyle remembered unhappily his days of traveling
and performing with Signor Valenti.
But in spite of everything, the two were
delighted to see each other once more.

In another part of the store, Mrs. Primm
searched frantically for Lyle.
"Excuse me," she said to the lady at
the information booth, "have you seen a
crocodile going past? He was wearing a red scarf."
"No," answered the lady. "I have no information
about a crocodile wearing a red scarf."

INFORMATION

Paris
Salon

14 16

ON PARLE FRANCAIS
AQUI SE HABLA ESPAÑOL
SI PARLA ITALIANO

"Excuse me," said Mrs. Primm to the sporting goods salesman, "have you by chance come across a crocodile? His name is Lyle."
"Sorry, madam," answered the salesman, "I have not come across any crocodiles named Lyle today."

Mrs. Primm grew more and more upset.
"Excuse me," she said to a man wearing a white carnation, "I have lost my crocodile and I don't know what to do."
Whatever the man answered, Mrs. Primm never heard it, for his voice was lost in a chorus of other voices shouting, "More, more!"

Those voices belonged to the huge crowd of shoppers
surrounding Hector P. Valenti and Lyle.
Because they had an audience, and because Signor
Valenti could not resist showing off, he had
persuaded Lyle to join him in a free performance
of their old stage act.
"More, more!" the surprised, but delighted
shoppers called out, forgetting all about
wanting or even needing pajamas.

Mrs. Primm caught up with them just in time
to hear still another voice, charged with fury,
shout, "What is going on here?"
This was Mr. Grumps.
And when Mr. Grumps saw what was really going on
his face turned red, blue and purple with rage.
"Madam," he gasped, "we do not permit crocodiles
in this store you know. Remove him at once!!
And you sir," he said, pointing a daggerlike finger
at Signor Valenti, "you sir, are dismissed!!"

"Something will have to be done about that crocodile."
Those warning words of Mr. Grumps still rang in
their ears as they said goodbye to Signor Valenti
outside the store.

Mr. Grumps at last made good his threat to do something about "that crocodile."
The next day he appeared at the Primms' door with papers authorizing Lyle to be committed to the city zoo.
"The zoo!" Mrs. Primm exclaimed miserably, "whatever would Lyle be doing in the zoo?"
"He'll be doing whatever it is normal crocodiles are supposed to be doing," snapped Mr. Grumps who wasn't being at all nice about it.
The Primms examined the papers.
They appeared to be in order.

There was little they could do, at least for the moment,
to prevent Mr. Grumps from putting Lyle in the zoo.

Lyle's first night
was difficult indeed.

Not wanting to seem unsociable, he decided
to join the other crocodiles
who were cozily piled together.
Just when he thought he had gotten
himself comfortable on top . . .

he awakened to find himself crushed to the very bottom.

Lyle's restlessness so annoyed the other crocodiles,
they all just got up and stomped off in a huff.

Lyle was happier during the day, when visitors
came. He amused everyone with his unusual tricks
and before long was the biggest attraction at the zoo.

Joshua and Mrs. Primm visited regularly,
arms laden with games, toys and the Turkish
caviar Lyle so loved.
Mrs. Primm did her best to smile
and appear cheerful, but just couldn't hide
her concern.
"Are you feeling all right dear?" she would ask.
"Are you getting enough rest?
Are you making friends with the
other crocodiles?
Do the lions keep you awake at night?
Is the floor too damp?
Do the flies pester you?"
Lyle shook his head yes or no, depending on
the question. He tried putting on a brave
front, but Mrs. Primm knew very well he was
unhappy and fought back her tears.

One night a new keeper appeared at Lyle's cage.
Surprise! Surprise!
The new keeper turned out to be
none other than
Hector P. Valenti, star of stage and screen.
"Sh!" whispered Signor Valenti,
"I have come to rescue you."
Signor Valenti unlocked the door of the cage
and an astonished Lyle was set free.

"You can't go home again," said Signor Valenti
when they had put the zoo behind them.
Signor Valenti was bursting with ideas.
"We'll put our old act together again," he said.
"We'll fly to Australia. They'll love us in Australia."
Lyle groaned. The very thought of never seeing the
house on East 88th Street again was grim indeed
and too much for him to endure.

Signor Valenti read his thoughts and decided
Lyle should have one last look at the house on
East 88th Street.
Approaching the now sleeping street, they were
suddenly met with a wall of dense smoke.
The smoke, they realized with horror, was coming
from Mr. Grumps' house.
While Signor Valenti ran to signal the alarm,
Lyle broke into the house and rescued the
still sleeping occupants.

A gasping, frightened Mr. Grumps and his cat
were led to the safety of the street.

Now the Primms and the entire neighborhood were awake
and witness to Lyle's heroism. Mr. Grumps
couldn't thank him enough.

"Ladies and gentlemen," said Mr. Grumps to the crowd
of onlookers, "Lyle is the bravest, kindest, most
wonderful crocodile in the whole, wide world. I would
consider it a privilege and a pleasure to have him
as our neighbor once more."

"Hooray!" shouted the Primms.

"Hooray!" shouted the crowd.

45

Lyle moved back to the house
on East 88th Street that very night.

Several days later, a farewell party was given
by the Primms for Signor Valenti, who was leaving
to seek fortune and adventure in Australia.
"Remember," said Mr. Grumps, speaking to Signor Valenti,
"should you change your mind about leaving, a job in
my store will always be yours just for the asking.
We need people with your kind of talent and ability."
Everyone smiled happily . . .

. . . even Loretta.